JOHN

THE SECOND CHILD

John Boyne was born in Ireland in 1971. He is the author of five previous novels, including the international bestseller *The Boy in the Striped Pyjamas*, which won two Irish Book Awards, was shortlisted for the British Book Award and has recently been made into a Miramax feature film. His novels are published in over thirty languages. His sixth novel, *Mutiny on the Bounty*, will be published in 2008. He lives in Dublin.

www.johnboyne.com

NEW ISLAND *Open Door*

THE SECOND CHILD
First published 2008
by New Island
2 Brookside
Dundrum Road
Dublin 14

www.newisland.ie

Copyright © 2008 John Boyne

The right of John Boyne to be identified as the author of this work has
been asserted by him in accordance with the Copyright, Designs and
Patents Act, 1988.

A CIP catalogue record for this book is available from the British
Library.

ISBN 978-1-905494-82-8

New Island receives financial assistance from
The Arts Council (An Chomhairle Ealaíon), Dublin, Ireland.

Printed in Ireland by SPRINT-print Ltd.
Cover design by Artmark

1 3 5 4 2

Distributed By:
Grass Roots Press
Toll Free: 1-888-303-3213
Fax: (780) 413-6582
Web Site: www.grassrootsbooks.net

Dear Reader,

On behalf of myself and the other contributing authors, I would like to welcome you to the sixth Open Door series. We hope that you enjoy the books and that reading becomes a lasting pleasure in your life.

Warmest wishes,

Patricia Scanlan.

Patricia Scanlan
Series Editor

One

The car pulled up outside the house just as Peter passed the window. He stood behind the curtains, peeping out. He sighed. He wished the visit was already over and he could be left in peace. His old car looked cheap beside the sleek BMW pulling up next to it. When he heard Annie, his wife, coming down the stairs, he stepped away from the window quickly.

'That's not them already, is it?' She rushed to the mirror and ran a brush through her hair. 'I thought we had another half hour yet.'

Peter grunted. He could smell her perfume in the air. It reminded him of Sunday mornings, endless sermons and good lunches.

'Now, you are to behave yourself, Peter Clarke,' she said. 'Do you hear me?'

'Don't be at me,' he muttered. He hated when she spoke to him as if he was a child. It made him realise that his marriage had fallen into three stages. The first was the early years, when there had been just the two of them. He had romanced her and she had enjoyed it. The second was when Dara and Alison were children. He had been tough because a family needed someone to take charge of things. Annie had been afraid of him then and with good reason. The third was now, when he was old and she was in control. They had swapped roles after one of his turns. He had never won his place back.

'I mean it,' she said. He nodded to shut her up. A knock came on the door. Annie rushed across to open it. Mother and daughter stood there in silence for a moment. They wore broad smiles. Peter stared at the ground. Nick stood in the driveway, switching on the car alarm out of habit. Then there were kisses to be given and greetings to be exchanged. At last they poured into the kitchen, their suitcases littering the floor.

'It's great to meet you at last, Mrs Clarke,' said Nick, putting out his hand. He had the whitest teeth she had ever seen. 'You too, Mr Clarke,' he added, shaking Peter's hand. The older man shook it for only a moment, silently, before letting it fall.

'Well, it's wonderful to meet you,' said Annie, a little star-struck. Her hand went to her hair to tidy it again. A blush made its way along her cheeks. 'We are so glad that you could make the trip.'

'Wouldn't have missed it for the world.'

Peter barely looked at him. He was busy trying not to stare at his daughter's large belly, the sign of the fifth month of a pregnancy. Annie had already warned him to keep quiet. She had threatened holy murder if he started any trouble. But looking at his daughter now, he felt ashamed and embarrassed for her. He noticed the way Nick kept one hand on the small of Alison's back. He didn't like it.

'And look at you,' said Annie. She reached across and placed a hand against her daughter's stomach. 'You look so healthy. Doesn't she look healthy, Peter? But how are you feeling? Are you eating all right? Are you sleeping?'

'I'm fine,' said Alison, nodding her head. 'A little tired maybe.'

'We took the morning flight and drove straight down from Dublin,' said Nick. 'It's not such a long drive to Wexford.'

'I thought you were flying in last night and staying over?'

'Nick had to work late,' explained Alison. She had almost changed her mind about this visit at the last minute. She had barely slept the night before with worry. 'So we switched to this morning.' It hadn't been her idea to come home. But there were only so many invitations that she could turn down without starting an argument When they were in Los Angeles it ha been easier. But since they had move to London there was no way out of And Nick had seemed so keen to co that she had finally agreed to the tri

'Well, sit down the pair of you,' ¦

Annie. 'I'll make some tea and you'll feel the life come back to you.'

'I might just go and wash first,' said Alison.

'Of course, of course. Nick, maybe you'd bring the bags up with you. Alison will show you the way.'

'Will do,' he said and they disappeared upstairs. Peter stood around nervously, feeling like a stranger in his own home. Annie stared at him and narrowed her eyes.

'Now, I'm warning you,' she said in a strict voice.

'Get on with your tea,' he muttered, turning away.

'She's five months pregnant, after all. I'm not saying I agree with it, but it would be mad to separate them.'

'Well, you know what I think.'

'I do. So don't start or there'll be a fight.'

Two

Over tea, Alison told them about the Los Angeles doctor who had been treating her early in her pregnancy. He had just been arrested for molesting some of his patients. It was the big story in California right then, she said. The doctor's patients included some big film stars. The ones who had suffered were pouring their hearts out on the TV talk shows. The ones who hadn't were looking for other types of publicity.

'That's shocking,' said Annie. 'And did he not seem a bit odd to you?'

'Not really,' said Alison. 'He always seemed a little quiet, if anything.'

'Well, I hope you'll steer well clear of him now.'

'He has been arrested, Mother. Anyway, we'll be in London until the birth, so it's neither here nor there. I've found a new guy at the Portland.'

'You're staying there that long, then?' asked Annie, breaking into a smile. She calculated quickly in her mind. The first train left Wexford just before eight in the morning and got in to Dublin by half ten. At that rate she could be on a flight by noon and in London an hour later. That was easy, she thought. Not like Los Angeles. She wondered if her daughter might invite her to stay when the baby was born.

'I'm doing a play in the West End,' said Nick. 'A six-month run. Of course, my agents are going crazy. But it's sold out already, so what can I do? Anyway, it seems more sensible to have the baby there and settle down for a few months before going back to the States.'

'In England?' asked Peter, speaking for the first time since they had all sat down. 'You're going to have the baby in England?'

'Yes, Dad,' said Alison quietly, after a brief pause.

'But sure, that will make him English.'

'A multi-national,' said Nick, grinning. 'American father, Irish mother, English by birth.'

'What do you want to do that for?'

'Well, as I said,' repeated Nick, keeping the smile fixed on his face, 'with the play and everything—'

'There hasn't been a child in my family born in England that I can remember,' said Peter.

'I had a cousin who went to live in Cornwall,' said Annie. 'And she married a lovely man. It will be fine.'

'I know,' said Alison.

Peter sighed and poured himself another mug of tea. He reached for his pipe. As he started to clean it, Nick opened his mouth. He wasn't sure if he should say something or not. Alison placed a hand on his and shook her head.

'If you don't mind,' she said. She looked at her father and placed the other hand on her stomach. It was the first time she had looked directly at him since she had arrived.

'You can't smoke around a pregnant woman, Peter,' said Annie. He glared at her for a moment before setting the pipe aside. There was an uncomfortable silence. 'So tell us about this play, Nick,' said Annie. 'It sounds very exciting.'

'It's a great character,' he said. 'The kind of thing I haven't done before. A real up-and-coming playwright. A guy who wants *nothing* to do with film, which is, you know, very refreshing. There are just three actors in it. No props – it all relies on the dialogue. But it's got a lot of laughs in it too. I mean, I haven't done any theatre since high school. I'm scared as hell. But it's just the kind of challenge I think I need right now. I'll probably get ripped apart for it, but …' He shrugged as if he didn't really mind one way or the other.

'Isn't that amazing,' said Annie, not quite sure what he had meant by most of that. 'I still can't believe it, to be honest.'

'Believe what?'

'Well,' she said, 'I mean, when Alison first told us that you were friends I didn't really know what to make of it. It's like being part of another world.'

Nick nodded. 'Right,' he said. 'But I have to tell you, driving down today from Dublin, the peace and quiet here …?'

Annie noticed that his sentences tended to drift off and sounded like questions. He was full of wonder. Americans in Ireland always were.

'I could live in a place like this. I really could.'

'Could you?' asked Annie. 'That would be marvellous. Wouldn't it, Peter?'

'He means in theory, Mother,' said Alison. 'Not in practice.'

'How do you live in a place in theory?' asked Peter.

Another silence followed. Nick laughed a little before stopping himself and staring down at the table. He tapped his fingertips on the wood and then stared at it.

'We have some news of our own,' said Annie finally.

'What's that?' asked Alison.

'I can't tell you,' she said.

'But you just—'

'Wait till your brother gets here. He'll tell you.'

'Well, where is he then?'

'He's still at work. He'll be home for his dinner. But we've a couple of hours before that yet. Nick, would you like to take a turn around the farm? Alison, why don't you show him around or bring him on a walk down to the village. I think I could use another litre of milk if you're going there.'

'What's the news you have?'

'Dara will tell you,' Annie said.

Alison sighed. 'Fine,' she said. 'Do you want to see the farm?' She looked across at her boyfriend.

'Sure,' replied Nick. 'Why not?'

'Come on then,' she said, standing up. 'What time should we be back?'

'No later than seven,' said Annie. 'Which gives you plenty of time for a nice walk. If you make it as far as the village, you can even have a drink before

13

dinner if you want. Oh, what am I saying?' she added quickly, remembering her daughter's pregnancy. 'You can't drink.'

'Tell me about it,' said Alison, turning away.

Three

During the whole conversation, Alison had felt her father's eyes burning into her. She had done everything she could not to look at him. He had said very little. And the only time she had spoken to him was to tell him that he couldn't smoke in his own house. He was dressed as she remembered him, in an old blue suit with an ancient pullover under it for warmth.

Their relationship had not always been so difficult. He had been a tough father. But he had doted on his daughter, his second child. Annie had once been jealous of the bond between them. He was forever telling Alison how much he loved her and that he would never let anyone hurt her. *You can tell your old dad anything*, he had often said. *Anything at all, any time, because I'll always be your old dad.* And she had taken him at his word, which was why they never spoke any more.

Alison had left the house eight years earlier when she was seventeen years old. It had caused a scandal in the village. She came home from school one day and had a conversation with her father. The father who had promised her that she could tell him anything. Then she had packed a bag for Dublin. She phoned from time to time. She even found time to write letters. But she had refused all invitations for Christmas or holidays

16

ever since. Annie had been to visit her a few times. But they never spoke of why she had left. Alison acted as if nothing had happened because she didn't want them to worry.

Eventually she had found work at a small film studio in Dublin. That had led to another job in London. Then it was on to Hollywood, where she had met Nick. They had fallen in love quickly and deeply. They had been together for almost three years. And now they were having a baby. She had waited a few weeks after finding out before phoning home to tell them the news. When she did, it was Peter who had answered the phone.

'Dad, hi, it's Alison.'

'There you are.'

'Is Mum there?'

She told Annie about the baby. Then her mother had told Peter. He said that they should marry or disgrace themselves. Annie said that, whatever they did, they would do it in their own time. People were different now. Nobody made such a fuss about these things any more. Besides, she didn't want any trouble. Not on this visit.

Four

There were two distinct groups in the pub that night: the old people and the young people. But they all stared at Alison and Nick when they walked in. The three old men sitting at the bar knew Alison was Peter's daughter. The one who had gone off to America and whose name was never spoken around her father. But they tipped their caps to her out of respect for Peter. They didn't like the look of her. Her clothes weren't fit for her. Her tan wasn't a Wexford tan. Not to mention the fact that a girl in the family way shouldn't wear a top like that. She should be trying to hide her shame, not show it off. They muttered greetings at her before turning back to their drinks.

The young people were a different matter. There was a group of about six of them from the local Spar. They ranged in age from fifteen to twenty-one. They sat at a long table with pints of beer and bags of crisps in front of each of them, even the youngest. It was a Thursday evening and they had just been paid. They always had a few drinks there before playing darts at the Lodge. Two of the girls had changed out of their red work shirts and white slacks. The rest still wore their uniforms. They had been laughing about something when Alison and Nick walked in. But their entry made them all stop and stare.

This sudden silence always happened when they entered public places. Alison and Nick had grown so used to it that they barely noticed any more. Alison sat down at a small table by a window. She looked out at the little stream running through Blackwater village. The tiny house on it had fascinated her as a child. Dara had once thrown her in the stream there. Since then she hated to go near water. She still didn't much like swimming.

This pub was the one where she had first taken a drink.

The shop across the road was where she had worked on Saturdays and half-day Sundays when she was a teenager.

Further along, in the church grounds, was where Paul Doyle had told her it was all right. He had said he wouldn't go all the way, that he would stop in time.

Past the stream was the bench where they had sat and she had felt angry with him. He had said it wasn't his fault. He said that once he had started there was no way of stopping. He hadn't meant to, honestly.

And over in the corner of this very bar was the table where they had sat a month or two later. He had said there was nothing he could do about it anyway. She had got herself into this mess. She could get herself out of it, he had said. And she had done that. She had stood up, gone home, talked to Peter about it, packed a bag and left.

'They seem pretty nice,' said Nick, sitting down. He handed her a glass of red wine. He placed a pint of Guinness on the table for himself. 'You're sure about that?' he asked, nodding at the wine.

'I'm sure,' she said, smiling and taking a sip. 'One glass of red from time to time is fine. The doctor said so. Anyway, I need it to take the edge off.'

'OK,' he said, tasting the Guinness. He frowned, not liking the stale taste of the hops and the warmth of the pint. He didn't drink much – it was bad for his skin. But when he did, he drank ice-cold bottled beers. American. Nothing else. But when he was in other countries he liked to try to fit in. 'They were very welcoming.'

'They put up a good show,' she said with a shrug.

'The way you built them up, I didn't know what to expect.'

'They're acting. You of all people should know when someone's doing that.'

He nodded but stayed silent for a few moments. He wasn't the type of man to tell someone they couldn't feel how they felt.

'Your mother seems real happy.'

Alison laughed. 'The poor woman is on a knife edge. You can see it,' she said. 'She's trying to keep everything friendly between everyone. Did you notice how she kept glaring at my dad every time he looked like he was going to say something? He wasn't allowed to open his mouth.'

'I thought he seemed fine. A little nervous, maybe.'

'He hates this,' she said, tapping her stomach.

'No, he doesn't.'

'He does.'

'He didn't say anything about it.'

'I know. Not even congratulations.'

Nick sighed. He was used to her moods and sharpness whenever they talked about her father. He reached across the table and took hold of her hand. His fingers played with hers. She looked back at him and smiled, grateful for his touch.

'You're going to be difficult until we get back to Dublin, aren't you?' asked Nick.

'A complete bitch.'

He laughed and she felt a surge of love for him. As he held her hand she placed the other against her stomach. 'It's just us,' she said. 'Just the three of us. No one else.' Nick nodded. He liked that idea.

It became obvious that the kids at the other table were staring at them. Some were curious, some muttering to each other. Above it all, one suddenly hissed, 'I'm telling you, it's not. It couldn't be.' Nick sighed. Normally he hated moments like this. But here in Wexford, far away from anywhere people could want anything from him, it didn't seem so bad.

'Are they staring?' he asked, because he had his back to them. He always sat that way in public.

'With their mouths wide open. You'd better say hello or they won't stop.'

Nick nodded and turned around. He glanced across at the kids, raising a hand in greeting. 'Hey,' he said. 'Nice to see you all.'

'Oh my God!' screeched one of the girls. She put her two hands to her mouth, her face scarlet. 'I told you!' Alison looked out towards the stream again. This would take a few minutes. 'It's you, isn't it?'

'Yeah, I guess it is,' said Nick, smiling at them.

'What are you doing here?' asked one of the boys. The girl beside him slapped his arm.

'Holiday,' said Nick.

'Will you give us an autograph?' asked one of the girls.

'Sure.'

A few of them came over. He signed beer mats for them. They stared at him, their lives transported to another world for a few moments. The boys told him how much they loved his action movies. The girls said they had loved the one where he had played the gay guy with no legs. The one he won the Oscar for. He nodded kindly and ordered a round of drinks for them.

'You must be your one, are you?' asked one of the girls. Alison turned, realising that she was talking to her.

'Sorry?' she said.

'I read about you in a magazine. They said you were from here but none of us believed it.'

'Afraid so,' said Alison. 'Born and bred.'

'Jesus,' said the girl. 'How did you get out?'

Alison opened her mouth and tried

to answer. But the words wouldn't come. For a moment she considered telling this girl the truth – exactly how and why she had left Wexford.

Before she could say another word, Nick, like a real movie star, shook all their hands. He thanked them and turned back to Alison, indicating that they should go away now. They did, but they continued to stare at him. His life was about being stared at. It happened every time he left the house. He had long since learned to tune it out.

'We should be getting back soon,' said Alison, looking at her watch. 'She said no later than seven.'

'OK,' said Nick, finishing his pint. He was glad he didn't have to drink another one. 'You know, if it goes well we could always stay another day.'

'You're kidding, right?' she said.

'Well, it's up to you.'

'One night. That was the deal. She knows that, anyway. I've told her you have rehearsals.'

Nick nodded. 'Up to you,' he repeated. They stood up and put their jackets on. They said goodbye to the kids, who still couldn't believe that he was really there. They went outside and walked hand in hand up the hill towards home.

Five

They were six for dinner, not the expected five. Dara's news was that he was engaged. He was glad of the chance to introduce his girlfriend to his sister. His pleasure was nothing, however, compared to the excitement of his new fiancée, Jane, at meeting Nick. She couldn't speak when they were first introduced. And she was nearly trembling when he shook her hand. She annoyed Alison by looking her up and down and asking, 'How did you manage to snare him?' Dara, on the other hand, was less impressed. He had never been much of a film buff.

'You're an actor, right?' he asked as they settled down to eat. Nick nodded. It had been a long time since anyone had asked him that. 'What kind of an actor, then?'

'Well, mostly action movies so far,' he said. 'Big-budget ones, you know. But I'm trying to expand my range. That's why I'm in London. Doing some theatre. We are all at it these days.'

'I don't much like the films,' said Dara. 'I can't sit still that long. My arse goes numb.'

'Jesus, Dara, what are you like?' asked Jane, embarrassed. She then listed Nick's credits, commenting on each one and the actors Nick had worked with. 'What's he like?' she asked. 'He seems very big on himself.'

'No, he's very nice. Very professional.'

'And her? I'd say she's a right stuck-up cow, is she?'

'She's lovely. Very sweet.'

'And what about himself? Is he gay? Everyone says he is.'

'I don't know about that. Sorry.'

For someone who claimed to love films, Jane seemed to dislike most of the people who acted in them. 'But how on earth did you two meet?' she finally asked Alison. She looked as if the idea of a girl from Wexford becoming involved with a famous movie star was about as likely as life being found on Mars.

'I was working as an assistant on a movie,' explained Alison. 'We met in the cafeteria. We were on location in Texas.'

'They let you talk to the stars?'

Alison smiled sweetly. 'If I promise not to use big words,' she said.

'Alison was more than just an assistant,' said Nick. 'The line producer was high most of the time. But his uncle was head of the studio so we couldn't get rid of him. Alison pretty much did his job.'

'Line producer,' said Jane in awe. 'I don't even know what that is.'

'It's when—'

'Peter used to take me to the pictures in the old days, didn't you, love?' said Annie. Her husband looked up from his plate.

'What's that?' he asked, surprised.

'The pictures. Do you remember back when we were courting? You used to take me to Gorey to the picture house there. We saw *Roman Holiday*, I remember,' she added, turning to Nick and putting her fork down. 'And *The Bells of St Mary's*. And *All about Eve*. You're probably too young to remember them, I suppose.'

'No, I love those movies,' he said.

'I loved Audrey Hepburn and Ingrid Bergman,' said Annie with a smile. 'And Gregory Peck, of course. He was wonderful. So handsome. They don't make them like him any more. Oh!' she said quickly, putting a hand to her mouth. 'Oh, I'm sorry, Nick. I didn't mean to suggest that you're not—'

'It's all right, Mrs Clarke,' he said, laughing. 'You're right anyway. They absolutely don't.'

'But you are very good,' she added quickly. 'I mean, I haven't seen many of your films. But Alison tells me you're very successful.'

'He makes twenty million dollars a movie,' said Jane, bobbing her head up and down. Alison closed her eyes and breathed in as the room went silent.

'Jane, don't be silly,' said Annie after a long pause. 'Twenty million dollars! The very idea.'

'It's true,' she insisted. 'You do, don't you?'

All eyes, except Alison's, turned to Nick. He looked embarrassed.

'You don't make that much money, do you?' asked Annie, shocked.

'Well, I guess …' he muttered.

'Twenty million dollars for making a film?' asked Dara, looking at Nick in awe. 'That can't be.'

'It's a funny business,' said Nick. 'But I'm only making a few hundred pounds a week for this play.'

Annie stared at him and then looked around the table. 'Did you hear that, Peter?' she asked.

'That's obscene,' said Peter in a clear voice. Nick laughed before realising that no one else was laughing, that Peter hadn't meant it as a joke. 'You should be ashamed of yourself,' he added after a moment.

'Dad, Nick's not responsible for

what he gets paid,' said Alison. 'That's the rate for the A-list.'

'You're on the A-list, are you?' asked Peter.

'He's near the top of it,' said Jane.

'And what the hell is an A-list when it's at home?' said Peter, ignoring her.

'It's not an actual list,' said Nick, looking uncomfortable.

'It's the names of the top box-office draws, Dad,' said Alison. 'As I'm sure you know. Eight or nine actors, a couple of actresses, people that can open a movie.'

'And tell me this, Nick,' said Peter. 'If you're on the A-list, where does that leave the likes of me?'

Nick opened his mouth and looked around for support. He wasn't used to being challenged on matters like this. He was thirty-seven years old. He had been working as a successful actor since he was sixteen. The things that surprised other people were his everyday life. They didn't seem so strange to him any more.

'Twenty million dollars,' said Dara, shaking his head. 'Why don't you just retire?'

'Well, what would I do?' asked Nick.

'Don't say that, Dara,' said Jane. 'You can't retire, Nick. You're brilliant!'

'When are you getting married?' asked Alison, changing the subject quickly.

Jane looked annoyed, as if she resented someone coming between her and the money. 'What's that?' she asked.

'I was asking if you had set a date yet.'

'April, twelve months,' said Dara. 'Please God.'

'You will be there, won't you, Nick?' asked Jane.

'Of course,' he said, nodding. 'And by then we'll have the baby too. We'll try not to have her crying in the church.'

'Her?' said Annie. 'Don't you mean him or her?'

'No, it's a girl,' said Alison, wishing Nick hadn't said anything.

'A girl? You found out already?'

'They do tests and if you want to know they tell you.'

'I wanted to get the nursery ready in time,' explained Nick. 'The designer needed to know so he could get the colours right.'

Peter laughed out loud and slapped the table with his hand. 'Well, that's the bloody limit,' he said.

'Dad,' snapped Alison.

'Dara, you should ask Nick to be your best man,' said Jane suddenly.

Dara stared at her in surprise, as did Nick.

'You what?' he asked.

'Nick,' she said. 'You should ask him to be your best man. He is your brother-in-law, after all. Sort of. The father of your niece.'

Dara looked at Nick with his mouth open. 'But I already asked Simon,' said Dara.

'Oh, don't mind Simon,' said Jane. 'Sure who is he, after all? He's nobody.'

'He's on the Z-list,' muttered Peter.

'He's my best friend,' said Dara. 'We've known each other all our lives.'

'But Nick is family,' said Jane.

'Do you have a big family?' asked Alison, trying to change the subject again.

'I didn't think … I'm sorry …' said Dara, looking at Nick. 'I mean, I suppose I could—'

'No, no, no,' said Nick quickly, shaking his head. 'Seriously, no. You ask your friend.'

'But if you'd expected—'

'I can promise you it never even entered my head,' said Nick.

'Oh my God! Oh my God! Oh my God!' said Jane suddenly, holding her hands out in the air. 'We could sell the pictures to a magazine. Can you imagine it? And they'd pay for the whole thing. We could upgrade!'

'Really,' said Nick, wishing he was far, far away, 'I couldn't expect—'

'Simon's already talking about the stag—' said Dara.

'We could have the wedding in Dublin then and—' said Jane

'Will you shut up, you stupid bloody girl,' shouted Peter, making them all jump. 'The lad has already asked his friend and he's only just met this fella. How could he ask him to be his best man, in the name of God? And let's be clear on one thing too: he's not family.'

'Dad,' said Alison quietly.

'Well, he's not, is he? Or did you get married without telling us?'

Nick shrugged. 'Well, no,' he said. 'We haven't got around to it yet. We are talking about it, but—'

'So you're bringing a child into the world without the benefit of marriage. Well, who needs morals when you're on the A-Team. Is that how it is?'

'The A-*list*,' said Jane.

'That's rich coming from you,' said Alison, ignoring her.

'What's that?'

'And I don't appreciate being told to shut up,' said Jane. 'Or being insulted in front of Nick.'

'I'm going to fetch the desserts,' said Annie, seeing all her plans beginning to fall apart. 'Nick, will you help me?'

'Sure,' he said, standing up quickly, grateful for an escape.

'And you needn't be running away, woman,' said Peter. 'Not twenty-four hours ago you said the same thing. You were the one talking about a double wedding.'

'We're not getting married,' said Alison.

'I didn't mean it,' said Annie. 'It was just idle chatter.'

Nick gathered the plates quickly and made for the kitchen door.

'You must really like Nick if you want us to get married,' said Alison. 'I mean, considering you only just met him.'

'It's not Nick that I'm worried about. It's that bloody baby,' said Peter. 'That's not how I brought you up.'

'Well, I know that to my cost, don't I?'

'Ah,' he grunted, looking away from her.

'I don't need your advice, Dad,' said Alison. 'Not this time.'

Peter's eyes narrowed as he looked at her. His hand gripped his fork tightly. His knuckles grew white. 'You be careful, girl,' he said in a low voice. It was enough to frighten her. She stopped herself from saying anything else.

'Alison, you'll help us, won't you?' asked Annie, returning to collect the gravy boat. She headed back towards the kitchen, where Nick was in hiding.

'I think I'll have a lie down if it's all the same to you,' said Alison, standing up. 'I feel a little ill.'

'Yes, then, you do that,' Annie said, pleased that one of the fighters was leaving the ring. 'I'll bring you up a cup of tea in a few minutes.' She fled into the kitchen. Nick was filling the sink with hot water and loading in the plates. 'Oh, you don't have to do that,' she said quickly.

'I want to. Honestly. I'd like to help. That was a fantastic dinner, Mrs Clarke.'

Annie nodded, but she wasn't in the mood for compliments. She started making tea. They said nothing to each other for a few minutes.

'I'm sorry about that,' said Annie finally. 'Peter and Alison. They haven't always been so difficult with each other, you know.'

'Hey, she's pregnant,' said Nick. 'Five months gone. Don't worry about it.'

'You must be careful with your own daughter. Don't let her … Well, they're not ideal with each other – you can see that.' Nick nodded but didn't reply. He felt it wasn't his place to comment. 'Can I ask you something?' said Annie after a moment. The tone of her voice made Nick stop what he was doing. He turned around and looked at her.

'Sure,' he said.

'Is she happy about the baby?'

'About it being a girl?'

'No, about it in general. Is she glad she's pregnant?'

Nick laughed. 'Are you kidding?' he asked. 'She's over the moon. It's all she ever talks about. I've never seen a woman want a child more.'

'Really?' Annie looked confused.

'Yeah. She has been reading books, getting the house ready. She has even organised monthly meetings with other mothers in the film industry. She wants all the babies to know each other. She was born to be a mother.'

'*Really?*' asked Annie again. 'When she talks to me on the phone, I always think …'

'What?'

'Oh, it doesn't matter. I'm probably wrong.'

'Tell me,' he insisted.

'Well, I always think she doesn't want her father or me to have anything to do with it. When I asked her could I come and help her out when it was born, she told me no. She wasn't even very nice about it.'

'I'm sorry,' said Nick, who had not heard about this. 'But you shouldn't take it personally. She is all over the place right now.'

'No, it's more than that. I feel like I'm being punished for something that I don't even know I did. Does that make sense?'

Nick nodded and put his arms around Annie and kissed her cheek. She blushed but was delighted. 'We *are* going to get married,' he said. 'Between you and me. We just don't want to make a big deal about it. With the world I'm in … well, it just turns into a circus once you start telling people.'

'Then you should do it here,' said Annie.

'What?'

'You should speak to the priest here, set a date. Don't tell a soul and just do it.'

Nick laughed and thought about it. He frowned as if he was trying to think of a good reason not to but couldn't come up with one. 'Well, we'll see,' he said in the end.

Six

When she woke, the room was pitch dark. In Los Angeles, even in London, there was always brightness streaming in from somewhere. There was always noise, the cars driving by, the sirens of police cars and ambulances. She lay still for a moment on her back. It was the only position where she felt comfortable now. She felt Nick's body beside her, curled up against her. He had one leg stretched across her own, the way he always slept. She edged closer to him, trying not to wake him.

She needed to feel his warmth in this familiar but strange place. She reached down and stroked his thigh. He moved nearer to her.

This was the room she had grown up in. It held many memories. Most signs of her time here had been taken away over the last seven years. She thought of her life for a moment, of the things that had happened to her since leaving Wexford. She thought of the man she loved lying beside her. It was all a long way from what she had imagined for herself growing up. But for a moment here, in the darkness after dawn, there was a peace that existed nowhere else. For that, she was grateful. She felt unexpectedly happy and considered waking Nick up to tell him. But she decided against it. If he woke now, they would only make love. She was starting to find that too uncomfortable. Instead, she tried to return to sleep. But her body and the baby had other ideas. She needed the bathroom. She slipped out of bed quietly, trying not to disturb the twenty-million-dollar man. She wrapped her robe around her and stepped outside.

The hallway was dark too. But she had spent enough years in this house to find her way around easily. By the time she came out of the bathroom, she felt hungry and wide awake. She went downstairs to see what was in the fridge. It was all she could do not to shout in surprise when she saw her father sitting by the fire. He was staring into the embers. He had just put in a piece of coal and it was starting to take.

'You startled me,' she said, almost laughing with the fright. 'What are you doing up at this time of night?'

'I might ask you the same question,' he said quietly.

'I spend half my life in the bathroom these days,' she said. 'Four more months of this.'

He nodded and looked back at the fire. Across from him was another armchair. She wanted to sit down but couldn't make the first move. 'I'm going to make a cup of tea,' she said. 'It might send me back to sleep. Do you want one?'

'I'll have one if you're making one,' he said.

'Right,' she said, slipping past him into the kitchen. She was grateful for the few minutes it would take to boil the kettle and make the tea. It would give her a chance to decide what to do next. Clearly she would be expected to sit and talk to him. But that was something she had not done in seven years. She wasn't sure this was the moment for it. But then again, she could hardly take the tea back upstairs to her dark bedroom. That would be a slight even she couldn't make. She decided to wait and see what her father said.

'There you are,' she said, handing him his mug.

'You'll sit down?' he asked quietly. It was an order framed as an question. She nodded and settled into the armchair. They sat together and looked at the fresh coal. Its black corners were starting to fizzle into red.

'I miss this,' she said after a few moments. 'A real coal fire.'

'You don't have one?'

'We have a fire and a hearth in the house in LA. But you just have to pull a rope and it blazes up. It's not real. The same one in New York and London. Nothing is real there.'

'The things they think of,' said Peter, shaking his head.

'I mean, we don't have to clean it out, of course,' she said, trying to drag out the easy conversation a little longer. 'That's a bonus.'

'And even if you did, I suppose you'd have a maid or someone to do it.' Alison said nothing. He was right, of course. 'I always found it relaxing,' he said after a moment. 'In the mornings. Sweeping out the hearth, taking out the ashes, setting it again.' She might have believed him except that she had never seen him do that. The household chores were not part of his daily routine. Her mother did them. 'With all that money, you should invest in one,' he added.

'We wouldn't be allowed,' she said. 'You couldn't release all that smog into the air. You'd be arrested.'

Peter laughed. 'So we don't have it so bad here after all,' he said.

'No,' said Alison.

'That's a queer amount of money to make, all the same, isn't it?' asked Peter, sounding curious now. 'You don't earn like that, do you?'

'God no,' she said with a grin. 'Not even a tiny bit of it.'

'I thought Jane was going to eat your fella alive. I thought we'd have to turn the hose on the poor girl.' Alison laughed and even Peter smiled at what he had said. 'I don't think young Dara would have had a look in.'

'No. He has that effect on people. It's very odd.'

'Well, you would know.'

Alison frowned. 'What does that mean?' she asked.

'Nothing at all. Only that he must have had an effect on you too. When you first met him, I mean. Considering you're both here now.'

She thought about it. She searched

through his words for any kind of insult. She was sure there was one in there if she looked hard enough. But she couldn't find it. Maybe he hadn't meant anything rude. Maybe he was trying to be friendly.

'Well, he won me over all right,' she said finally. 'But it took time. I'm a tough nut to crack.'

Peter looked his daughter in the eyes before looking down at her belly. Then he raised an eyebrow. 'Really?' he said flatly.

'Yes, really,' she said. She looked at her stomach herself when he looked away. 'Do you have something to say about this?'

'Sure, I've nothing to say. I'm only making conversation.'

'Right. Well, that makes a change.'

'Does it now?'

'Yes, it does.'

'Ah right.'

She bit her lip and remembered this stubborn streak. She knew she had it too. The way her father would happily pick a fight with anyone who offended him. But try to get him to face up to his own hypocrisy and you might as well be trying to get whiskey from a coconut.

'Still,' she said. 'At least this child won't be born here.'

'No, you said. You're having the poor creature in England, for her sins.'

'Oh, please.'

Peter put his pipe down and looked across at her. He sighed. 'Is there something you want to say to me, Alison?' he asked. She blinked. This was a new tactic – being direct. It put her off her game for a moment. 'Because this is me, a man sitting in his own chair, by his own fire, in his own house. And it's just the two of us here. So if you have something to say, you might as well just spit it out. Then you can stop acting like I'm the devil.'

She thought about it but shook her head. All the things she had dreamed of saying over the years. All the times she had wanted to go back to that day, when she had told him her news because he was the one she trusted. He was the one who had said she could tell him anything. Now he was offering her the chance again.

'Does he know?' asked Peter finally.

'Nick?'

'Yes. Does he know about what happened?'

Alison nodded. 'Of course he knows,' she said.

Peter shrugged in surprise. 'Really? I didn't think he did,' he said. 'I didn't think you'd have told him.'

'He doesn't judge people.'

'That must be a nice thing to be able

to afford. And he doesn't hold it against you?'

Alison stared at him as if he was crazy. 'Why would he?' she asked. '*You* might have held it against me. But you can't judge other people by your standards.'

'No, I realise that,' he said. His tone suggested that, while she might feel others had higher standards than him, for her father it was the other way around.

She stood up. 'I had better get back to bed,' she said.

'You know he died, do you?' asked Peter.

She stopped and stared at him. 'Who died?' she asked.

'Himself. The Doyle fella.'

'He died?' she gasped, sitting down again. She hadn't heard.

'A car crash. Three years ago this

October. They say he was drunk and went into a tree. His poor mother and father were beside themselves.'

Alison felt a little sick. He would only have been twenty-three then, she realised. He would have died in Wexford the same time she met Nick in Texas. How two lives can go in such separate directions, she thought. 'Why didn't you let me know?' she asked.

'That's your mother's job.'

'Well, why didn't she let me know? She knows we … went out.'

'I told her that I'd tell you. And then I told her you didn't want to talk about it again.'

'Really?' she asked. 'Why would you do that?'

'I didn't think you'd want to be reminded of him.'

'That's not true. I liked Paul.'

'He was half a man.'

'He was a kid.'

'He was a little bastard who got what was coming to him.'

Alison shook her head. 'It wasn't him that drove me away,' she said. 'It wasn't him who left me with no choices at all.'

'Well, it wasn't me if that's what you mean.'

'It is.'

'I had nothing to do with it,' he said in an even tone. He shifted the coals of the fire with the poker.

'I came to you …' she began. The words were so heavy inside her that it was like carrying a dead weight. 'I came to you with—'

'With what?' he snapped. 'With what? With one of them?'

'You said I could tell you anything.'

'You couldn't have stayed here.'

'Why not?' she asked. 'Why couldn't I?'

'How would we have explained it?'

'Who cares?' she asked with a laugh.

He shook his head and settled down.

'Well, it doesn't matter now anyway,' he said. 'Sure, you've only gone and done it again. But now that you've got yourself a rich husband, you'll hold on to this one, I'd say.'

'He's not my husband.'

Peter snorted. 'No,' he said. 'And never will be. A man doesn't want a wife like that. A dirty creature.'

She said nothing for a moment and thought about it. She was too tired to fight. She didn't want to be there anyway. This wasn't home. Home was a place where you felt comfortable and safe. This was not that place. 'I'm going back to bed,' she said. 'We have to leave early in the morning.'

'Maybe I did wrong,' he muttered quietly when her back was turned. His voice was so low that she could barely hear him.

'What did you say?'

He was silent for a few moments, but she waited for him to speak.

'Everything was different then,' he said finally. 'I don't know,' he added with a sigh. 'Sure, things have worked out well for you anyway. I'm glad of that.'

'Did you say you did wrong?' asked Alison, amazed. She had heard the words. She had needed to hear them. But she wanted to be sure.

'What's that?' asked Peter.

'What did you just say?' she asked him. 'Say it again.'

Peter lifted his pipe again. 'Go on up to bed now,' he said quietly. 'You'll catch your death down here.'

She waited for more and then turned and walked slowly upstairs. She tried to decide if it was enough for her, him briefly admitting failure. Was it enough?

Seven

Alison looked at Nick and blinked. 'Sorry?' she asked. 'What did you say?'

'I said it would probably be easier if we stayed in a hotel next time,' he repeated. 'When we come back for the wedding, I mean.'

She nodded. 'Yes,' she said. 'Probably.' They were driving down the lane away from the house. She was watching the figures through the side mirror as they disappeared in the distance. Her mother waved. Dara stood beside Jane, who was taking photographs of the car as it sped away. Up ahead she could see her father walking down the lane towards the gates which he had offered to open for them. It was a task that his children used to fight over years before. She folded her arms as she waited for him to reach the end and open them.

'They're nice people,' said Nick. 'A little different to what I'm used to.'

'Except for Jane.'

'Yes, I'm used to that, that's for sure.'

'Poor Dara,' said Alison. 'He's not going to get a look-in at the wedding. It will all be about you and her. You want to be careful she doesn't get you to say the vows too.'

'We don't have to go.'

Alison stared at him. 'Yes, we do,' she said. 'He's my brother. And you're the best man, remember?'

Nick groaned. Dara had announced it that morning over breakfast.

Apparently Jane was getting her way after all.

'What happened last night?' Nick asked quietly.

'When?'

'Last night. I woke up and you weren't there so I went out into the hallway. I could hear you talking to your father.'

'You heard us?' Alison looked at him in surprise.

'I heard voices. You seemed to be in the middle of something so I went back to bed. Was everything OK?'

She sighed. She wasn't sure. 'This is just a difficult place for me to be,' she said. 'There are so many memories here.' She patted her stomach. 'It might be a while before we can come back.'

Nick shrugged. 'They're your family,' he said. 'It's up to you. We don't have to come back at all if you don't want to. They can always come and visit us.'

'If they have to.'

'They're going to want to see their grandchild.'

'Then I'd rather came to us.'

Nick nodded. Peter had opened the gates wide. He was standing by them, waiting for the car to drive through. 'Right,' Nick said. 'Dublin, here we come.'

He drove slowly out the gate, raising a hand to Peter, who ignored him. Alison stared straight ahead, her arms still folded before her. She was determined not to look at him. Finally, though, she couldn't help it. She glanced in his direction just as he turned away. For a moment she was sure he winked at her, like he used to do when she was a little girl. When she looked in the side mirror again, she could see the two heavy gates closing behind her. And there was the stooped figure of her father in his blue suit and old pullover. He was smaller now than she had ever realised. She watched him walk away and disappear back into the family home.

OPEN DOOR SERIES

SERIES ONE

Sad Song by Vincent Banville
In High Germany by Dermot Bolger
Not Just for Christmas by Roddy Doyle
Maggie's Story by Sheila O'Flanagan
Jesus and Billy Are Off to Barcelona
by Deirdre Purcell
Ripples by Patricia Scanlan

SERIES TWO

No Dress Rehearsal by Marian Keyes
Joe's Wedding by Gareth O'Callaghan
The Comedian by Joseph O'Connor
Second Chance by Patricia Scanlan
Pipe Dreams by Anne Schulman
Old Money, New Money by Peter Sheridan

SERIES THREE

An Accident Waiting to Happen
by Vincent Banville
The Builders by Maeve Binchy
Letter from Chicago by Cathy Kelly
Driving with Daisy by Tom Nestor
It All Adds Up by Margaret Neylon
Has Anyone Here Seen Larry?
by Deirdre Purcell

SERIES FOUR

The Story of Joe Brown by Rose Doyle
Stray Dog by Gareth O'Callaghan
The Smoking Room by Julie Parsons
World Cup Diary by Niall Quinn
Fair-Weather Friend by Patricia Scanlan
The Quiz Master by Michael Scott

SERIES FIVE

Mrs Whippy by Cecelia Ahern
The Underbury Witches by John Connolly
Mad Weekend by Roddy Doyle
Not a Star by Nick Hornby
Secrets by Patricia Scanlan
Behind Closed Doors by Sarah Webb

SERIES SIX

Lighthouse by Chris Binchy
The Second Child by John Boyne
Three's a Crowd by Sheila O'Flanagan
Bullet and the Ark by Peter Sheridan
An Angel at My Back by Mary Stanley
Star Gazing by Kate Thompson